# HOP, HOP, JUMP!

LAUREN THOMPSON

*illustrated by*

JARRETT J. KROSOCZKA



Margaret K. McElderry Books

New York • London • Toronto • Sydney

MARGARET K. McELDERRY BOOKS • An imprint of Simon & Schuster Children's Publishing Division • 1230 Avenue of the Americas, New York, New York 10020 • Text copyright © 2012 by Lauren Thompson • Illustrations copyright © 2012 by Jarrett J. Krosoczka • All rights reserved, including the right of reproduction in whole or in part in any form. • MARGARET K. McELDERRY BOOKS is a trademark of Simon & Schuster, Inc. • For information about special discounts for bulk purchases, please contact Simon & Schuster Special Sales at 1-866-506-1949 or business@simonandschuster.com. • The Simon & Schuster Speakers Bureau can bring authors to your live event. For more information or to book an event, contact the Simon & Schuster Speakers Bureau at 1-866-248-3049 or visit our website at www.simonspeakers.com. • Book design by Lauren Rille • The text for this book is set in Avenir. • The illustrations for this book are rendered in acrylic paints on illustration board. • Manufactured in India • 1011 MSS • 10 9 8 7 6 5 4 3 2 • Thompson, Lauren, 1962– • Hop, hop, jump! / Lauren Thompson ; illustrated by Jarrett Krosoczka.—1st ed. p. cm. • Summary: Rhyming text, accompanied by labeled illustrations that identify parts of the body, encourages readers to wiggle and twist, stomp and zig-zag, and hug and shrug. • [1. Stories in rhyme. 2. Exercise—Fiction] I. Krosoczka, Jarrett, ill. II. Title. • PZ8.3.T32522 Hm 2012 • [E] • 2011022544 • ISBN 978-1-4169-9745-0 (hardcover) • 978-1-4424-5802-4 (eBook)

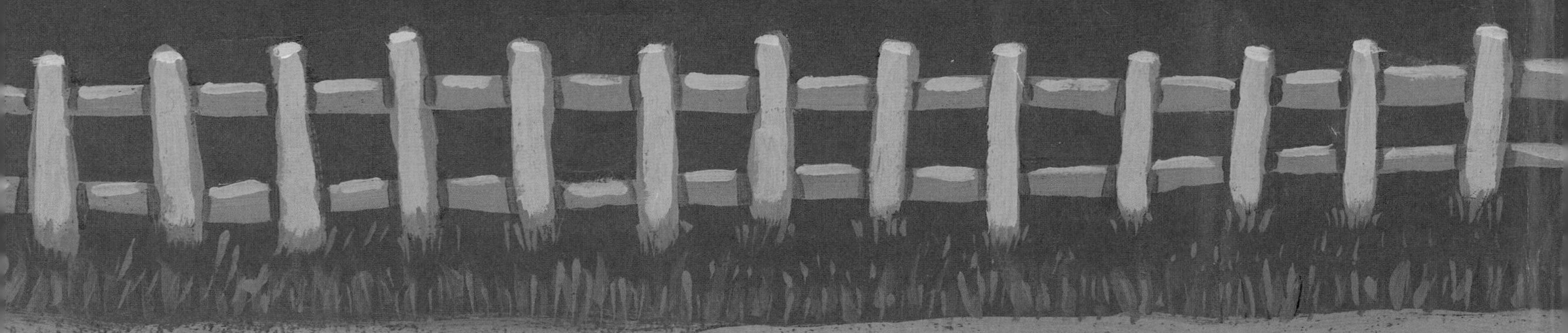

To Nina
—L. T.

For Rebecca Sherman,
a mover and a shaker
—J. J. K.

Move your body!
Have some fun!

Watch!
We'll show you how it's done.

Wiggle it.

Waggle it.

Wing it.
ELBOW

Wave it.

Upside-down it.

HEAD

Hop, **hop,**

# JUMP!

Squint it.

Grin it.

Shrug it.

Hug it.

LEG

# STOMP!

Goose it.

Groove it.

Reach it.

Roll it.

Twist it.

Kick it.

Flip, **flap,**

# FLOP!

It's your
turn now!

SHOW!

Take

a

BOW!